AIR FORCE

John Townsend

A⁺

Smart Apple Media

Published by Smart Apple Media, an imprint of Black Rabbit Books
P.O. Box 3263, Mankato, Minnesota 56002
www.smartapplemedia.com

Published by arrangement with Watts Publishing, London.

Cataloging-in-Publication Data is available from the Library of Congress
ISBN: 978-1-59920-985-2   (library binding)
ISBN: 978-1-68071-000-7   (eBook)

Picture credits:
Cody Images: 6l, 8, 9b, 19, 21t, 25, 27, 28.
Flight Collection/Topfoto: 23b.
The Granger Collection/Topfoto: 14t.
Hulton Archive/Getty Images: front cover.
Khomenko/RIA Novosti/Topfoto: 16.
Library of Congress: 11, 12, 13.
The National Archives/HIP/Topfoto: 4t, 5, 9t, 15b.
Picturepoint/Topham: 1, 4c, 6r, 10, 23t, 29.
RIA Novosti/Topfoto: 17tr.
Roger-Viollet/Topfoto: 18.
Topfoto: 17, 21b, 24.
ullsteinbild /Topfoto: 7, 22t, 22b.
US Navy: 20.
Anatoly Sergeev-Vasiliev/RIA Novosti/Topfoto: 17tl.
Wikipedia: 19cr.

Every attempt has been made to clear copyright. Should there be any inadvertent omission please apply to the publisher for rectification.

Printed in the United States by CG Book Printers
North Mankato, Minnesota

PO 1727
3-2015

Contents

War in the Air

World War II (1939—1945) was the first war to send hundreds of thousands of advanced aircraft into combat. With such air power, the war was like no other, as planes attacked anywhere behind enemy lines, including *civilian* as well as military targets. This was very much everyone's war.

BACK THEM UP!

All air forces in World War II held recruitment drives.

ACTION STATS

Aircraft Available in Europe in World War II

Date	British	US	Soviet	Total Allied	German
June 1942	9,500	—	2,100	11,600	3,700
December 1942	11,300	1,300	3,800	16,400	3,400
June 1943	12,700	5,000	5,600	23,300	4,600
December 1943	11,800	7,500	8,800	28,100	4,700
June 1944	13,200	11,800	14,700	39,700	4,600
December 1944	14,500	12,200	15,800	42,500	8,500

Aircraft were important for attack, defense, and reconnaissance (information gathering). Studying *aerial* photographs helped the planning of many ground operations.

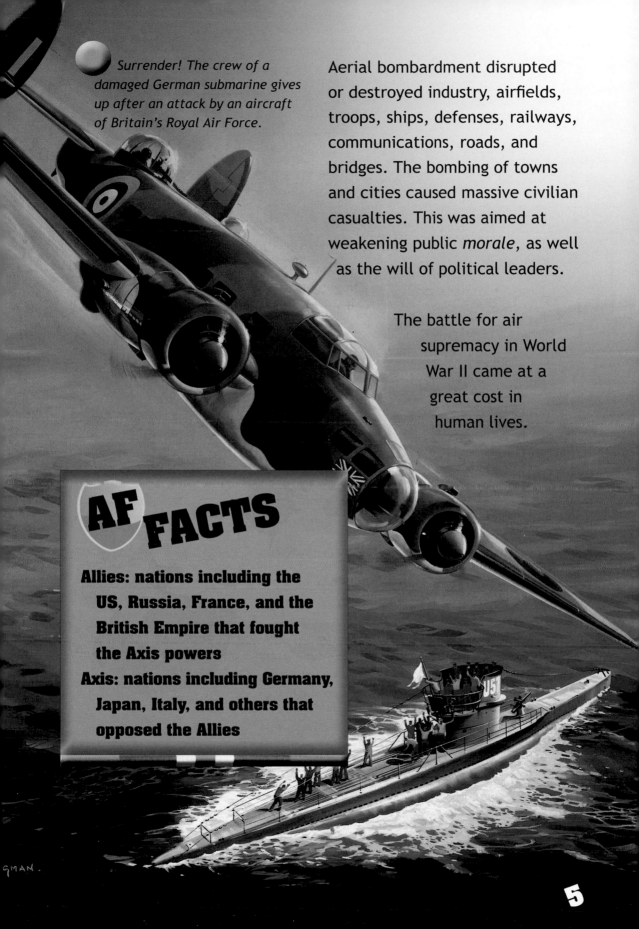

Surrender! The crew of a damaged German submarine gives up after an attack by an aircraft of Britain's Royal Air Force.

Aerial bombardment disrupted or destroyed industry, airfields, troops, ships, defenses, railways, communications, roads, and bridges. The bombing of towns and cities caused massive civilian casualties. This was aimed at weakening public *morale*, as well as the will of political leaders.

The battle for air supremacy in World War II came at a great cost in human lives.

AF FACTS

Allies: nations including the US, Russia, France, and the British Empire that fought the Axis powers

Axis: nations including Germany, Japan, Italy, and others that opposed the Allies

Hitler's Air Force: The *Luftwaffe*

In 1934, Adolf Hitler became the leader of Germany. He and his Nazi Party rapidly began building up the country's military strength, including its air force.

By 1935, the *Luftwaffe* (German air force) was established, and thousands of new aircraft were built. Commanded by World War I pilot Hermann Goering, the Luftwaffe became the largest and most powerful air force in Europe by the start of World War II in 1939.

Nazi leader Adolf Hitler (left) and Luftwaffe chief Hermann Goering (right).

Germany began World War II by invading Poland in September 1939, with the Luftwaffe backing up the *Wehrmacht* (German ground forces) with 1,200 fighter aircraft and 1,750 bombers. The main German aircraft were:

Messerschmitt Bf109: a key modern fighter plane with mounted machine guns and/or cannons;

Junkers Ju87 Stuka: a two-man (pilot and gunner) dive bomber and ground-attack aircraft;

Dornier Do17: a "light bomber" with crew of four: the pilot, a bomb-aimer, and two gunners;

Heinkel He111: a fast "medium bomber" with a crew of five.

A formidable weapon. Heinkel He111s flying in formation.

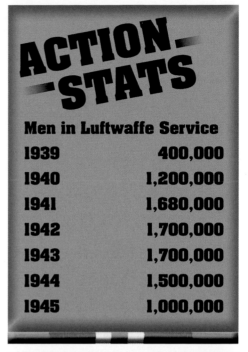

ACTION STATS

Men in Luftwaffe Service	
1939	400,000
1940	1,200,000
1941	1,680,000
1942	1,700,000
1943	1,700,000
1944	1,500,000
1945	1,000,000

AF FACTS

Luftwaffe comes from the German words *Luft* "air" and *waffe* "weapon" or "arm." One of the Luftwaffe's main tactics was to use surprise air strikes to back up attacking ground forces.

The Royal Air Force

The massive Nazi aircraft-building program of the 1930s meant that Britain's Royal Air Force (RAF) lagged behind. When war broke out in 1939, the RAF was catching up, but it suffered heavy losses at the beginning of the war as it fought against more advanced German aircraft.

ACTION-STATS

Key RAF fighter aircraft:

Supermarine Spitfire
Introduced in 1936, the Spitfire was a modern single-seat aircraft armed with machine guns. The MkV model had a maximum speed of 375 mph (605 km/h).

Hawker Hurricane
Like the Spitfire, the Hurricane was fast and *maneuverable*. Both fighters had powerful Rolls-Royce engines.

Restored World War II Spitfires fly over England.

As Germany invaded other European countries such as Belgium and France, RAF bombers attacked the advancing German army but were often outgunned and outmaneuvered. British and French armies were forced to retreat, with almost 200,000 British soldiers and 140,000 French being rescued by boats from Dunkirk while under attack by the Luftwaffe. The RAF fought back but with serious losses; 177 of its aircraft were shot down, including 106 Hurricanes and Spitfires.

Facing heavy losses, the RAF asked the US for extra pilots and planes. The first year of World War II was the darkest of times for the RAF.

This World War II poster attempted to boost morale by boasting of the RAF's strength.

RAF pilots relax at an airfield between missions. A Hurricane fighter sits behind them, ready to fly.

9

Fighter Aircraft

Unlike bombers and attack aircraft that strike ground targets, fighter aircraft are designed for air-to-air combat with enemy planes. They are built for speed and maneuverability.

At the start of World War II, the Luftwaffe's feared Messerschmitt Bf109 was the key fighter in air battles over France. It was designed in the 1930s, and was the first modern fighter with a closed *canopy*, a powerful liquid-cooled engine, and retractable landing gear.

The Bf109 could reach a maximum speed of 400 miles per hour (640 km/h) and had a range of 530 miles (850 km) before needing to refuel.

The RAF's legendary Spitfire had a shorter range of 470 miles (760 km), but it could climb higher than its rival in combat.

Having shot down a German Dornier Do17 bomber (left), an RAF Hurricane sweeps away to look for a new target.

P-51 Mustangs are prepared for testing near a factory in California.

Some fighter aircraft were designed to escort bomber aircraft to and from their targets. They had to be able to fly long distances without refueling and to fight off enemy attacks on the bomber formations.

The American P-51 Mustang was often used as an escort fighter in World War II. Armed with machine guns, bombs, and rockets, it carried a huge fuel load and was one of the best all-round fighters of the war.

Bombers

Throughout World War II, air forces constantly developed bigger and better aircraft to carry bigger bomb loads. There were three kinds of bombers:

Light Bombers: These planes carried a bomb load of 1,100-2,200 pounds (500-1,000 kg). They were used for short bombing missions and also for *reconnaissance* work. The United States supplied the RAF with the Lockheed Hudson and Martin Baltimore light bombers.

An A-20 Havoc bomber makes a test flight.

Medium Bombers: These could carry larger bomb loads of 99,000-220,000 pounds (45,000–100,000 kg) for longer distances than light bombers. The United States built over 7,000 Douglas A-20 Havoc medium bombers during the war. These were used by many Allied air forces.

The De Havilland Mosquito was a British medium bomber used in high-speed missions attacking factories and other targets in Germany and occupied Europe.

AF FACTS

Dive bombers, such as Germany's Junkers Ju87 Stuka, would dive in a swarm from 14,700 feet (4,500 m) to a release *altitude* of 3,000 feet (900 m) in about 30 seconds. Their accuracy made them much feared in air raids.

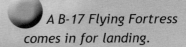

A B-17 Flying Fortress comes in for landing.

ACTION STATS

12,000 heavy bombers were shot down in World War II. Between 1939 and 1945 the Allies dropped 3.4 million tons (3.1 million t) of bombs.

Heavy Bombers: These four-engined aircraft were used chiefly by the US and Britain. The US's B-17 Flying Fortress was the world's first four-engine long-range heavy bomber. The RAF's Avro Lancaster became famous for its use in the "dambuster" raids of 1943. Heavy bombers like these were used to smash the industrial centers of Axis countries.

Case Study: Battle of Britain

In the summer of 1940, Hitler planned to invade Britain. The Luftwaffe increased bombing raids on British cities in the *"Blitz,"* but also set out to destroy the RAF in aerial combat.

ACTION STATS

The Blitz lasted from September 7, 1940, to May 21, 1941. British cities targeted by the Luftwaffe included London, Birmingham, Liverpool, Plymouth, and Glasgow. Over 40,000 people in Britain were killed in air raids, but in the end the Blitz was a failure—Britain didn't surrender!

AF FACTS

**Battle of Britain
Date: July–Oct 1940
Place: The skies above
England
Code Name: Operation
Sealion (the name
given by Hitler to Nazi
Germany's planned
invasion of Great
Britain)**

Spitfires of the RAF engage German bombers heading for British cities in the Battle of Britain.

"Never in the field of human conflict was so much owed by so many to so few."

WINSTON CHURCHILL

This poster uses British Prime Minister Winston Churchill's famous words to celebrate the courage of RAF pilots.

Throughout August and September, the Luftwaffe's attacks continued. Despite being outnumbered, the RAF fought back with increasing success. There were heavy losses on both sides. The Luftwaffe then concentrated on bombing cities rather than aerial combat. This gave the RAF's exhausted crews time to recover.

By October, the Luftwaffe was losing the battle because its fighters had only limited time for flying over Britain before they ran out of fuel and ammunition. Germany lost the Battle of Britain—the first major Axis defeat of World War II—and called off the invasion.

Soviet Air Force

One reason that Germany lost the Battle of Britain was because Nazi leaders were concentrating their efforts elsewhere. They were focusing on the east and planning Operation Barbarossa: the invasion of Russia.

Russia's air force (the VVS) was quickly training pilots and ground support crews but they still weren't ready when Germany attacked in June 1941. Despite suffering many losses, the Soviet "Red Air Force" had three powerful aircraft:

ACTION STATS

In the first few days of Operation Barbarossa, the Luftwaffe destroyed 2,000 Soviet aircraft, most of them on the ground—with only 35 Luftwaffe aircraft lost.

• **The Ilyushin Il-2** was a fast two-man dive-bomber with armor to withstand direct hits. It was known as the "Flying Tank," and the Soviets built 36,000 of them during the war. Its two cannons and two machine guns, as well as a 1,450-pound (660-kg) bomb load, made it a powerful plane for supporting Russian ground troops.

Side and top views of the versatile Ilyushin Il-2.

- **The Petlyakov PE-8** bomber had a long range and it could reach targets inside Germany.

- **The Yakovlev Yak-1** single-engine fighter was effective in attacking the Luftwaffe at close range.

The Yak-1 was maneuverable, fast, and well armed.

AF FACTS

One thousand Russian women volunteered to become pilots. Three entire regiments were made up solely of women who regularly flew on bombing raids. The most famous was Lilya Litvyak (pictured), known as the "White Rose of Stalingrad." She shot down 22 enemy aircraft before she was shot down herself.

Japanese Air Force

While the war in Europe spread, Japan was building its air power so it could take over areas around the Pacific Ocean. By 1941 the Japanese Army Air Force had about 1,500 aircraft ready to attack land targets, while the Japanese Navy Air Force had more than 1,400 planes.

Fearing the United States would try to stop its plans for Pacific domination, Japan sent a huge force of aircraft to attack the US fleet at Pearl Harbor in Hawaii, on December 7, 1941.

In just two hours 18 US warships, 188 aircraft, and 2,403 servicemen were lost in the attack. Both the US and Japan had entered World War II.

Japan's air force had many successes, but the growing strength of US air power led to Japan losing air supremacy. In late 1944 the Japanese used a surprising new tactic: the *kamikaze* suicide plane. Japanese pilots began crashing their aircraft into US ships. Many kamikaze pilots were only 18 to 24 years old. Most believed killing themselves for Japan was a very honorable thing to do.

A young Japanese kamikaze pilot poses for his last photograph.

An attacking kamikaze aircraft heads straight for a US ship in the Pacific.

The Japanese Mitsubishi A-6 "Zero" fighter was an outstanding aircraft.

AF FACTS

The first Japanese kamikaze attack was in October 1944. A Japanese plane flew straight into an Australian navy ship, killing 30 sailors.

ACTION STATS

By the end of the war over 2,500 Japanese pilots had killed themselves on kamikaze missions. About 5,000 US and Allied sailors died in kamikaze attacks.

US Air Power

As soon as the US joined the war, it launched air attacks against Japanese bases in the Pacific. The first US air raid to strike Japan itself was in April 1942, when 16 B-25 bombers took off from the aircraft carrier USS *Hornet*.

Bound for Tokyo, a B-25 bomber takes off from the deck of the USS Hornet.

Their bombs caused little damage and the planes, which had no way of returning, were lost. Three crew members died and eight were captured. Despite this, the raid shocked Japanese people and leaders, who had thought they were beyond the range of US bombers. It also boosted US morale after the disaster at Pearl Harbor.

Wildcats were also used by Britain's Royal Navy. They are shown here on the deck of the carrier HMS Formidable.

A US Navy aircraft carrier could hold nearly twice the aircraft of a similar-sized Japanese carrier. The Grumman F4F Wildcat was very short and had folding wings—perfect for storing on the decks of aircraft carriers. Its successor, the faster and sturdier F6F Hellcat, could outfight Japanese Zero fighters. A short burst from its six machine guns was usually enough to bring down a Zero.

Hellcats on a mission.

21

Jet Power

World War II saw the development of the first jet aircraft. Powering planes with jet engines provided far greater speed for swifter attacks.

Messerschmitt Me262 in camouflage paint. One German pilot said flying it was "as though angels were pushing."

Both Britain and Germany were developing jet engines at the start of the war. However, it was the German Messerschmitt Me262 that became the world's first operational jet-powered fighter. In the last year of the war, it shot down many Allied aircraft. Germany also built the Heinkel He162 jet fighter (below), but metal was so scarce that the plane had to be made mainly of wood.

ACTION STATS

Luftwaffe's Heinkel He162 jets could reach a speed of 560 miles per hour (900 km/h), but could only fly for 30 minutes before refueling.

The V-1 Doodlebug had a single engine mounted at the rear of the craft.

In 1942, America's first jet fighter, the Bell XP-59, was tested. The US Army Air Corps was not impressed by its performance, so production stopped and it never went into combat.

However, the Allies did use Britain's first jet fighter, with *turbojet* engines developed by Sir Frank Whittle. The Gloster Meteor first flew on missions in July 1944 with the RAF's 616 *Squadron*. The squadron's first mission was to attack V-1 flying bombs. By January 1945, Meteors were stationed in Belgium, supporting Allied ground forces as they fought their way to Berlin.

The Gloster Meteor's top speed was more than 550 miles per hour (900 km/h).

Night Raids

Many air force missions took place at night. Aircraft were obviously safer if they couldn't be seen by the enemy below, but there were risks in flying in the dark. Aircraft in World War II didn't have satellite navigation systems, so finding targets and not getting lost were real problems.

No night-fighter aircraft existed at the start of World War II. Pilots feared searchlights and anti-aircraft guns. Air forces developed night fighters designed especially for air combat in the dark. *Radar* was one of the important systems for guiding pilots in low visibility.

Lancaster bombers of the RAF on a night mission to bomb Germany.

AF FACTS

The Northrop P-61 Black Widow was the first US military aircraft designed especially for night attacks using radar. The first test flight was in May 1942 and its first missions were in 1944.

The P-61 Black Widow had a distinctive twin-boom tail design.

ACTION STATS

Lancaster Bomber

Length:	69 ft. 11 in. (21.11 m)
Wingspan:	102 ft. (31.09 m)
Bomb load:	13,889 lb. (6,300 kg)
Firepower:	Eight machine guns
Top range:	2,531 miles (4,073 km)
Power:	Four engines
Crew:	7

RAF Bomber Command sent many night raids over Germany, using Lancaster bombers to target the Luftwaffe's aircraft factories. By July 1943, German night fighters were having a success rate of 5 percent shooting down RAF bombers. Night fighters used radar to find them in the dark. To jam enemy radar, bombers dropped thousands of aluminium strips called "chaff." These clouds of metal pieces not only confused radar systems, but they also puzzled people living below when it rained aluminum!

Case Study: Battle of the Philippine Sea

Landing aircraft at night on moving carriers in the middle of the ocean was treacherous. It proved deadly for American pilots not trained to land in the dark when returning from a major air battle in the Pacific in 1944.

The battle was the last of five between Japanese and American aircraft carriers at the Mariana Islands. It was also a major defeat for Japanese forces.

During the battle, 77 US dive-bombers, 54 torpedo planes, and 85 fighters took off from American carriers in Task Force 58 to attack the Japanese fleet. Hundreds of Japanese planes from nearby bases flew into the battle, but over 350 of them were shot down on the first day.

AF FACTS

The Battle of the Philippine Sea
Date: June 19–20, 1944
Place: The Mariana Islands (Pacific Ocean between Japan and New Guinea)
Nickname: Great Marianas Turkey Shoot

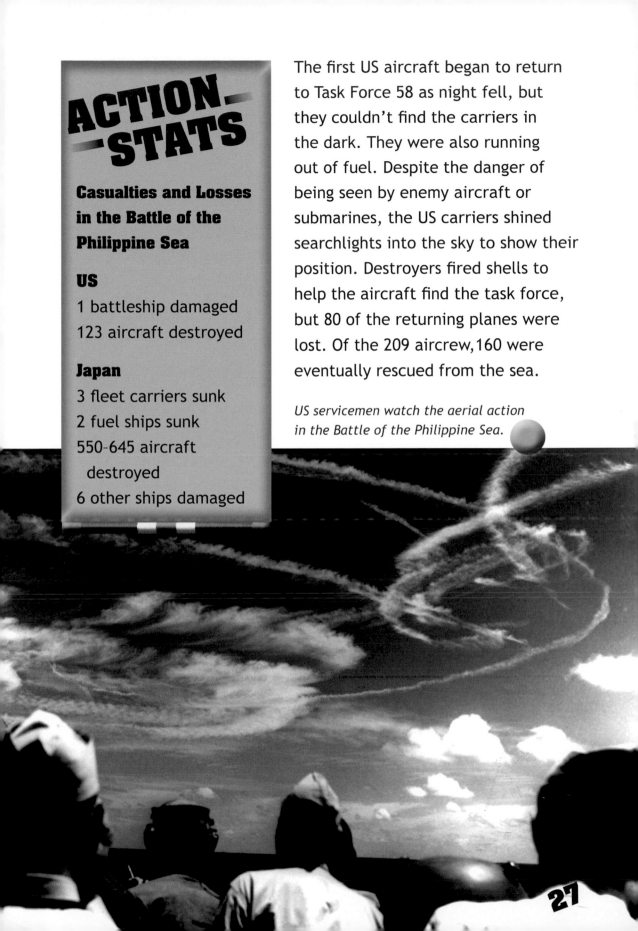

ACTION STATS

Casualties and Losses in the Battle of the Philippine Sea

US
1 battleship damaged
123 aircraft destroyed

Japan
3 fleet carriers sunk
2 fuel ships sunk
550-645 aircraft
   destroyed
6 other ships damaged

The first US aircraft began to return to Task Force 58 as night fell, but they couldn't find the carriers in the dark. They were also running out of fuel. Despite the danger of being seen by enemy aircraft or submarines, the US carriers shined searchlights into the sky to show their position. Destroyers fired shells to help the aircraft find the task force, but 80 of the returning planes were lost. Of the 209 aircrew, 160 were eventually rescued from the sea.

US servicemen watch the aerial action in the Battle of the Philippine Sea.

Final Air Assaults

On D-Day (June 6, 1944), Allied troops landed on French beaches to begin freeing Europe from the Nazis. Allied air forces engaged in major attacks to further weaken the Luftwaffe's airpower.

Eventually the Allies advanced to Berlin, Germany, where air raids continued to weaken Nazi morale. The Luftwaffe was outnumbered, out of fuel, and defeated. The war in Europe was finally over in May 1945.

The war with Japan continued for another three months until the US bombed its cities like never before. When Japanese leaders refused to surrender, the US sent a Boeing B-29 Superfortress bomber with an atomic bomb on board.

Colonel Paul Tibbets in the cockpit of Enola Gay, *the aircraft that dropped the first atomic bomb on August 6, 1945.*

It dropped the first ever bomb of its kind on the Japanese city of Hiroshima, causing huge destruction. Three days later, Japan's leaders had not surrendered, so the US dropped another atom bomb, this time on the city of Nagasaki.

Japan eventually surrendered and the Allies celebrated VJ (Victory in Japan) Day on August 15, 1945—although the surrender wasn't signed until September 2. World War II was finally over after six devastating years and the most intensive air campaigns in history.

AF FACTS

VJ Day marked not only the end of the war in the Pacific, but also the end of World War II. In Britain, huge crowds gathered to cheer King George VI and Prime Minister Winston Churchill, while the RAF provided the triumphant flypast!

An exhausted US airman celebrates VE (Victory in Europe) day beside his aircraft on May 8, 1945.

NAZIS QUIT!
Doenitz Gives Ord

World War II Timeline

- 1939: September 1 – Germany invades Poland. Great Britain and France declare war against Germany.

- 1940: Luftwaffe engages the RAF in the Battle of Britain, then attacks British cities in the Blitz.

- 1941: December 7 – Japan bombs Pearl Harbor, bringing the US into the war.

- 1942: April – 272 RAF bombers attack Hamburg, Germany at night—the largest raid yet on a single target.

- 1942: July – The first US B-17 Flying Fortress arrives in the UK.

- 1943: January – The RAF attacks Berlin, Germany for the first time with Mosquito aircraft.

- 1943: October 14, Black Thursday – Nearly 600 crew members are lost in an Allied bombing raid on a factory in Germany.

- 1944: March – Allies bomb Berlin, dropping thousands of tons of bombs, with heavy losses on both sides.

- 1944: June 6 – After a nighttime air assault, over 160,000 Allied troops land along the Normandy coast on D-Day.

- 1944: June 19-20 Battle of the Philippine Sea – US fighter planes help defeat the Japanese fleet.

- 1945: April 10 – Allied aircraft shoot down half of the German Messerschmitt Me262 jet fighter planes. The loss is fatal to the Luftwaffe and their defense of Berlin is abandoned.

- 1945: April 30 – Adolf Hitler commits suicide in his bunker, and within days Germany surrenders.

- 1945: August 6, 9 – US drops atomic bombs on Japan.

- 1945: August 15 – Japan surrenders, officially ending World War II.

Glossary

aerial – operating from aircraft in the sky

altitude – the height of an aircraft above the ground

blitz – a sustained series of air raids

canopy – the sliding cover that shields a pilot inside an aircraft's cockpit

civilian – ordinary member of the public who does not belong to the armed forces

dogfight – a battle at close range between fighter planes

kamikaze – in World War II, attacks in which Japanese pilots loaded their aircraft with explosives and crashed into enemy targets

Luftwaffe – the German air force before and during World War II

maneuverable – able to turn, climb, and dive quickly while in flight

morale – the mood and state of mind of a person or group

radar – stands for radio detecting and ranging – using radio waves for locating objects

reconnaissance – a mission to gain information about the enemy

retractable – able to be pulled in. Retractable landing gear/wheels retract into the wings or body of a plane to improve air speed

squadron – a working unit in an air force consisting of aircraft, the pilots to fly them, and the ground crew to look after them

turbojet – a jet engine using a turbine to compress an air-fuel mixture in a combustion chamber. A spark ignites the mixture and this creates a jet of hot gas that pushes the aircraft forward

Index